For Michael with all my love

First published in Great Britain in 2009 by Bloomsbury Publishing Plc.
Published in the United States of America in 2009 by Walker Publishing Company, Inc.
Visit Walker & Company's Web site at www.walkeryoungreaders.com

For information about permission to reproduce selections from this book, write to
Permissions, Walker & Company, 175 Fifth Avenue, New York, New York 10010

Library of Congress Cataloging-in-Publication Data
Gliori, Debi.
Stormy weather / written and illustrated by Debi Gliori.
p.   cm.
Summary: As nighttime approaches, a baby fox and his mother imagine
all the different animals around the world preparing for bed and falling asleep.
ISBN-13: 978-0-8027-9419-2 • ISBN-10: 0-8027-9419-X (hardcover)
ISBN-13: 978-0-8027-9422-2 • ISBN-10: 0-8027-9422-X (reinforced)
[1. Stories in rhyme. 2. Bedtime—Fiction. 3. Foxes—Fiction.
4. Animals—Infancy—Fiction. 5. Mother and child—Fiction.] I. Title.
PZ8.3.G47St 2009   [E]—dc22   2008043523

Art created with watercolor and ink
Typeset in St Nicholas
Book design by Debi Gliori

Printed in Belgium by Proost
2 4 6 8 10 9 7 5 3 1 (hardcover)
2 4 6 8 10 9 7 5 3 1 (reinforced)

FSC
Mixed Sources
Product group from well-managed
forests and other controlled sources
Cert no. BV-COC-070303
www.fsc.org
© 1996 Forest Stewardship Council

This book is printed with vegetable inks

Stormy Weather

Debi Gliori

Walker & Company · New York

Pull up the quilt, turn out the light,
dear child, it's time to say good night.
In darkness black and soft and deep,
I'll watch beside you while you sleep.

Across the world
in many beds
a million bedtime
stories read

of frogs and kings
and gingerbread,
then lights go out,
good nights are said.

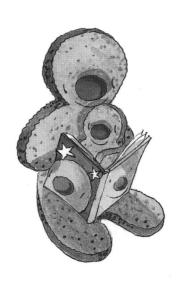

Then should the oceans roar and rise
and dark clouds race
across the skies

I'd hold you tight and close and warm
and keep you safe all through the storm.

If thunder tore the night in two
and lightning played at peekaBOO,

we'd watch the storm pass overhead,
then curl up safe and snug in bed.

And if that breeze became a gale—
whipped leaves, snapped twigs, made branches flail

I'd wrap you safely in my wings and tell you tales of sleepy things.

And if it rained ten thousand rains
and torrents swept down streets to drains,

we'd build a boat and sail away
to where the sun shines bright all day.

And if the snow began to fall,

flake on flake piled up so tall

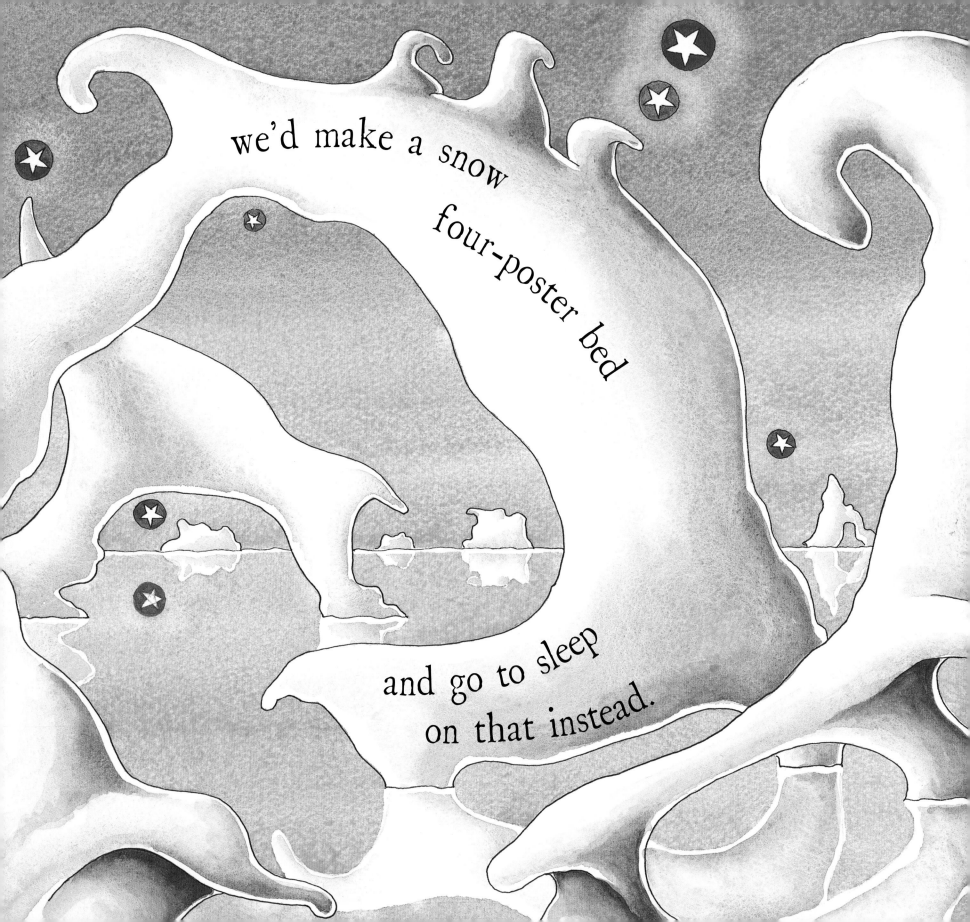

From north to south and east to west,
from cave to berg and twig to nest,
a sleepy hush across the world,
small creatures in their beds are curled.

Sweet dreams beneath our sheltering sky,
the tides and winds our lullaby,

the stars our light, the whole night through
shine down so bright on me and you.